THE
RAINBOW RIBBON

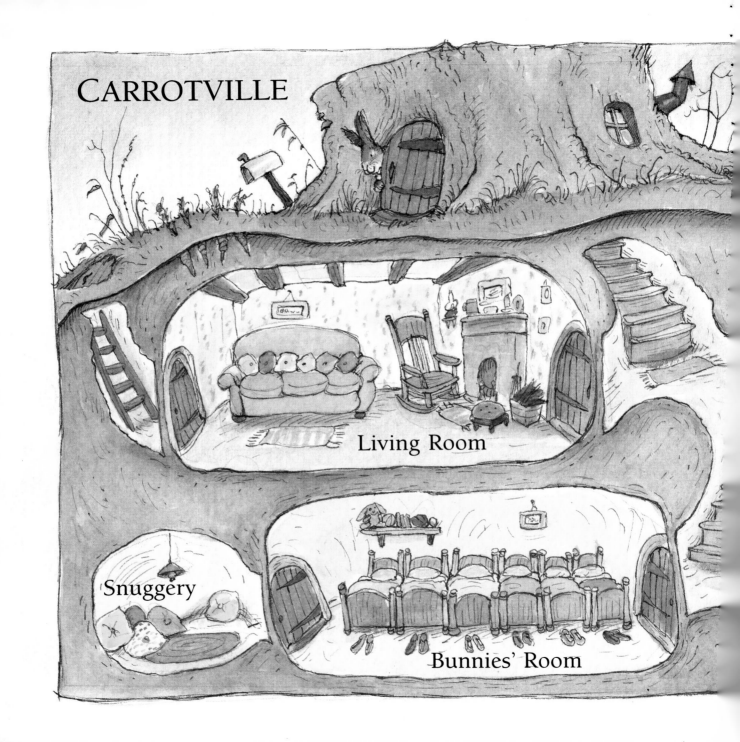

Attic

Dining Room

Kitchen

Mama's
Room

Rhoda   Ricky   Mama   Margaret   Rowdy   Rooter   Rena
Rabbit   Rose

THE RAINBOW RIBBON

A BANK STREET BOOK ABOUT VALUES

by William H. Hooks and Betty Boegehold

Illustrated by Lynn Munsinger

VIKING

VIKING
Published by the Penguin Group
Viking Penguin, a division of Penguin Books USA Inc.,
375 Hudson Street, New York, New York 10014, U.S.A.
Penguin Books Ltd, 27 Wrights Lane, London W8 5TZ, England
Penguin Books Australia Ltd, Ringwood, Victoria, Australia
Penguin Books Canada Ltd, 2801 John Street, Markham, Ontario, Canada L3R 1B4
Penguin Books (N.Z.) Ltd, 182–190 Wairau Road, Auckland 10, New Zealand

Penguin Books Ltd, Registered Offices: Harmondsworth, Middlesex, England

First published in 1991 by Viking Penguin, a division of Penguin Books USA Inc.

1 3 5 7 9 10 8 6 4 2

Series graphic design by Alex Jay/Studio J
Editor: Gillian Bucky
Special thanks to James A. Levine and Regina Hayes

Copyright © Byron Preiss Visual Publications, Inc., 1991.

Text copyright © The Bank Street College of Education, 1991.

Illustrations copyright © Byron Preiss Visual Publications, Inc., and Lynn Munsinger, 1991.

A Byron Preiss Book

Carrotville is a trademark of The Bank Street College of Education.

Library of Congress card catalog number: 00-00000

ISBN: 0-670-82866-1

Printed in Singapore

For Molly Elizabeth Davies—W.H.H.
For Julie—B.B.
For Andrea—L.M.

An old rabbit in a polka-dot jacket came hopping down the path to Carrotville.

Who'll buy my ribbons bright?

Blue, red, or snowy white?

Rainbow ribbons, purple, pink, or green?

The prettiest ribbons you've ever seen!

"It's Ribbon Rabbit! He's here!" called Rhoda.

All the rabbits rushed out to take a look at Ribbon Rabbit's wares.

Rowdy, Ricky, and Rooter looked at the ribbons. "Just stuff for girls," said Rowdy.

"Oh, Mama," cried Rhoda. "Let us buy some ribbons!"

"Please let us," begged Rena.

"I *want* a ribbon right now," shouted Margaret Rose.

"Hold your carrots," said Mama Rabbit. "I'll buy you some ribbons."

"Me first," yelled Rhoda.

"No, *me* first," said Rena.

"No, no, *me* first," cried Margaret Rose.

"Great jumping gerbils!" shouted Mama Rabbit. "Quiet! You can choose in alphabetical order!"

Margaret Rose bounced up and down.
"*M* for Margaret Rose comes before *R* for
Rena and Rhoda!" she cried. "So, I'm the first
to choose. And I choose red!"

Ribbon Rabbit pulled out a shiny ribbon,
red as lips, red as fire, red as a rose.
"Rosy red for Margaret Rose," he said.
"That's me!" shouted Margaret Rose.
"I always choose red."

Margaret Rose hopped around and around
chanting, "Red as a rose, for Margaret Rose!"

"Me next," said Rena, "because *Re* comes before *Rh*. I choose blue."

Ribbon Rabbit flipped out another shiny ribbon, blue as the sea, blue as the skies, blue as a baby's eyes. "Blue for a bunny named Rena," he said.

"I'm last," said Rhoda, "but I'll pick the best ribbon of all. I choose this rainbow ribbon that's green, yellow, orange, red, purple, and blue."

Ribbon Rabbit held up a shiny, shimmering ribbon and said, "A rainbow ribbon for Rhoda Rabbit."

Margaret Rose stopped chanting.
Margaret Rose frowned. "I want the rainbow
ribbon," she shouted.

"Too bad. It's mine," said Rhoda.

"Not fair! I didn't see it," said Margaret Rose.
"I'm taking the rainbow ribbon."

"Oh, no, you aren't," shouted Rhoda.

Margaret Rose began to cry. "It's not fair,"
she sobbed. "I won't live here anymore
if you are all so mean to me."

"No more about ribbons," said Mama Rabbit.
"Come, Ribbon Rabbit, let's have lunch.
Soup's on, everybody."

All the bunnies ran to the kitchen. All except Margaret Rose. She stopped crying.

She said, "They're so mean to me. If I'd seen that rainbow ribbon first, I would have picked it. It's really mine, so I'll go and take it."

Tippy-hop-tippy-hop, Margaret Rose stole into the living room, where the rainbow ribbon was lying on a chair. She put down her ribbon, and picked up the rainbow one and stuffed it in her pocket. Then, she went to the kitchen for soup.

Soon all the soup was gone.
Ribbon Rabbit hopped away singing:
> *Who'll buy my ribbons bright?*
> *Blue, red, or snowy white?*
> *Rainbow ribbons, purple, pink, or green?*
> *The prettiest ribbons you've ever seen!*

Rhoda and Rena went to get their ribbons.
Rhoda screamed, "Somebody stole my ribbon!"

Mama Rabbit rushed into the room.

"Mean, rotten Margaret Rose stole my ribbon
and left me her red one," sobbed Rhoda.

"Don't call your sister mean and rotten," said
Mama. "What did you do with the rainbow ribbon?"
she asked Margaret Rose.

Margaret Rose rolled her pink eyes and said,
"Who, me? What ribbon?"

"Give back Rhoda's ribbon," said Mama Rabbit.
"You had first choice. Fair's fair!"

But Margaret Rose didn't give back the ribbon.

"All right," said Mama Rabbit. "If you don't play fair, you must play by yourself. Go up to the attic, Margaret Rose."

"Who cares?" said Margaret Rose. "I like to play by myself." Thumpty thump, she stomped up to the attic.

Rowdy and Ricky and Rooter yelled up to the attic:

Margaret Rose, she's the one,
stole a ribbon, and away she runs!

Margaret Rose stuck out her tongue at them. "Didn't! Didn't! It's my ribbon. I'm not going to stay here. I'm going away forever!"

She thumped down from the attic, out of the house, and down the road. But pretty soon, she began to feel lonesome. Margaret Rose didn't like being alone, especially outside the house. She sat down on the grass. The rainbow ribbon felt heavy in her pocket.

Someone sat down beside her. It was Ribbon
Rabbit. "I'll give you all my ribbons,
if you give me something," he said.

"What can I give you?" asked Margaret Rose.

"Your family," said Ribbon Rabbit.
"You are going away forever, aren't you?
And you like ribbons better than your family, right?
I have no family, so it's a fair trade. Right?"

Margaret Rose's lip began to quiver. A big tear ran down her cheek. "I do like my family," she sobbed. "I like them better than ribbons. I'll give Rhoda her ribbon. I want to go home."

Margaret Rose stood up. "I know!" she said. "You come home with me, too. Then, we'll both have a family!"

"Leaping lettuce leaves!" cried Ribbon Rabbit. "What a terrific idea!"

So paw in paw, Margaret Rose and Ribbon
Rabbit hopped home together singing:
Rainbow ribbons, purple, pink, or green,
the prettiest ribbons you've ever seen!

Running away won't make things right.
It won't solve a problem or settle a fight.
It does no good to sulk and pout.
Home is the place to work things out.